Guru Nanak's Way: Less

Guru Nanak's Way: Lessons for Young Hearts

Aariv Wadhwa

Published by Aariv Wadhwa, 2024.

This is a work of fiction. Similarities to real people, places, or events are entirely coincidental.

GURU NANAK'S WAY: LESSONS FOR YOUNG HEARTS

First edition. November 7, 2024.

Copyright © 2024 Aariv Wadhwa.

ISBN: 979-8227453624

Written by Aariv Wadhwa.

Chapter 1: Curious Little Nanak
Chapter 2: The Secret of the River
Chapter 3: A Trade with Love
Chapter 4: Friends from All Paths
Chapter 5: The Smallest Bow
Chapter 6: The Honest Hands
Chapter 7: Treasures of the Heart
Chapter 9: The Kind Heart Challenge
Chapter 10: The Lion's Roar of Truth
Chapter 11: A Circle of Equals
Chapter 12: The Calm Stone
Chapter 13: The Gifts of Earth and Sky
Chapter 14: Wings of Forgiveness
Chapter 15: Walking Together

Long, long ago, in a small village nestled between green fields and rolling rivers, there was a gentle boy named Nanak. He had the warmest smile and the kindest heart, and even as a child, he saw the world a little differently. While others went about their day, young Nanak would look up at the stars and wonder, "Why are we here?" or watch the birds fly and think, "How do they know where to go?"

As he grew older, Nanak's gentle heart only grew wiser. He realized that life was full of secrets—a magic of love, kindness, and togetherness that could change the world. He wanted to share these secrets with everyone, so he set off on a journey, meeting people far and wide, spreading a message of peace, joy, and unity. Everywhere he went, he reminded people that all of us—no matter who we are or where we come from—are connected, like leaves on the same big, beautiful tree.

This book is a collection of the stories and lessons Guru Nanak shared on his travels. They are simple tales, but they hold treasures for young hearts like yours. Each story is a window into a world of kindness, courage, and wonder.

Are you ready to step into that world? Then, come along—let's walk the path of love and light together. This is Guru Nanak's Way. Let his journey inspire yours!

Chapter 1: Curious Little Nanak

In the small, bustling village of Talwandi, a young boy named Nanak was known to all. He wasn't like other children who would rush to play or be caught up in games of mischief. Little Nanak was thoughtful, kind, and, above all, *curious*. His eyes sparkled with questions about everything he saw, and his heart was full of compassion for everyone he met.

From the time he could speak, Nanak was always asking questions that seemed simple but held deep wisdom. The villagers often found themselves stumped by his questions, unable to answer this young boy whose mind seemed as wide and endless as the sky. His parents, Mehta Kalu and Mata Tripta, were both puzzled and proud of their young son. They saw how gentle he was and how he noticed things that others often overlooked.

One sunny morning, little Nanak was sitting by his mother, watching her cook food for the family. His big, curious eyes followed every move she made as she added spices, stirred the pot, and tasted the broth. After a few moments, Nanak's forehead wrinkled with a question.

"Mother," he asked, his voice soft but serious, "why do we cook so much food just for ourselves? There are so many people outside who might not have any food today."

Mata Tripta smiled at him, but she could sense that her son's question wasn't just playful curiosity. Nanak genuinely wanted to understand why their food wasn't shared with everyone. This wasn't the first time he had asked something so thoughtful, and she gently tried to explain. "Nanak, we have to take care of our family first," she replied. "But we also help others when we can."

Nanak nodded, but his mind was still full of questions. He wanted to know why some people had so much and others had so little. Why did some families have enough food to waste, while others went hungry?

Nanak's heart ached at the thought of people suffering while others were comfortable. Even at his young age, he felt the pain of others as if it were his own.

One day, while playing outside, Nanak noticed an elderly man sitting under a tree, looking tired and hungry. The man was a traveler who had come from a distant village, and his clothes were dusty from his journey. Nanak felt a tug at his heart, as he often did when he saw someone in need.

He quickly ran back home and brought out a small portion of his own lunch to offer the man. The man's eyes filled with gratitude as he accepted the food with trembling hands, and he blessed Nanak with a smile. Nanak's heart felt light and happy as he watched the man eat. It was a simple act, but it filled him with a warmth he had never felt before.

Later, when Nanak's father, Mehta Kalu, found out about the shared meal, he was puzzled. "Nanak," he asked, "why did you give away your food? That was meant for you."

Nanak thought for a moment before replying, "Father, the man was hungry. I already had enough to eat. Why should I keep more for myself when someone else is hungry?"

Mehta Kalu was both surprised and moved by his son's words. He realized that Nanak had a natural kindness that was rare, even among adults. Nanak's curiosity wasn't just about learning facts or knowing answers; it was a gentle urge to understand and ease the pain of others.

On another day, Nanak's father took him to the bustling village market. Nanak was thrilled to see the market's vibrant colors, sounds, and smells. There were stalls selling fruits, grains, spices, and fabrics. People haggled over prices, exchanged goods, and laughed together. But Nanak's keen eyes noticed something else.

At the edge of the market, he saw a group of children dressed in ragged clothes, their faces thin and tired. They looked on as others bought food and sweets, but they had nothing to spend. Nanak's heart felt heavy as he saw their longing faces. He tugged at his father's sleeve and whispered, "Father, why don't those children have anything to eat or wear? Why can't they buy the things they want?"

Mehta Kalu looked down at his son, unsure how to answer. "Nanak," he began, "life is different for everyone. Some people have more, and some have less. We can't help everyone."

"But why, Father?" Nanak asked, his eyes wide with a question that seemed to reach beyond his years. "Why do some have so much while others have so little? Isn't there enough for everyone?"

Mehta Kalu paused, realizing that Nanak's innocent question held a wisdom far beyond his age. He didn't have an answer that would satisfy his son, and he could only smile and gently pat Nanak's head. "You are still young, Nanak," he said. "One day, you will understand."

But Nanak didn't want to wait for that "one day." In his heart, he already felt that there must be a better way—a way where everyone could share and no one would go without.

One day, while playing with other children near the fields, Nanak noticed a sheep that had wandered away from its flock. The sheep looked frightened and lost, unable to find its way back. The other children giggled and chased the sheep, thinking it was a funny game, but Nanak watched with concern.

He slowly approached the sheep, speaking softly to calm it. "Don't worry, little one," he said gently. "I'll help you find your way back." The other children stopped and watched in surprise as Nanak led the sheep back to its flock with a steady hand.

When he returned, his friends asked him, "Why did you bother with that sheep? It was just a silly animal."

Nanak looked at them with a patient smile. "The sheep was scared and alone. Just because it's an animal doesn't mean it doesn't feel things. If we can help, why shouldn't we?"

His friends fell silent, thinking about Nanak's words. They began to see that kindness wasn't just about helping people; it was about caring for all beings, no matter how small or different.

One evening, Nanak sat with his family by the river, watching the water flow gently by. The sun was setting, casting a warm glow on everything around them. Nanak's mind was full of questions, as always, and he turned to his father with a serious look.

"Father," he asked, "why does the river keep flowing? It never stops, even when it's tired. Does it ever wish to rest?"

Mehta Kalu laughed softly, but Nanak's question lingered. "The river flows because it has a purpose," he replied. "It gives water to the land and helps plants and animals grow. It doesn't think about itself; it just keeps giving."

Nanak thought about this, realizing that maybe people could be like the river—always giving, always helping without thinking of themselves. It was a small thought, but it planted a seed in his heart that would grow into one of his most cherished beliefs: the importance of selfless service.

As Nanak grew, so did his questions and his desire to understand the world. His family and the villagers often found themselves amazed at the wisdom that came from this young boy. They began to see that his questions weren't just about learning facts but about understanding how to live with love, kindness, and fairness.

When someone asked Nanak why he cared so much, he would smile and say, "Because everyone is connected. When someone else is happy, I feel happy too. When someone is sad, I feel their sadness too. Aren't we all part of the same family?"

The villagers would often shake their heads, wondering how such wisdom could come from someone so young. Little did they know that this gentle, curious boy would one day become a great teacher and a guiding light for people around the world.

Chapter 2: The Secret of the River

It was an early dawn in Talwandi, and the village lay quiet under the soft, golden light of the morning sun. Birds chirped in the trees, and the river glistened like a ribbon of silver in the distance. This was Nanak's favorite time of day—the world felt still, and everything seemed connected in a silent harmony. Today, he decided to visit the river alone, following the path that led through fields of wildflowers and tall grasses swaying in the gentle breeze.

The river held a special place in Nanak's heart. It was where he would sit for hours, watching the water flow, listening to the gentle murmurs of the current. He loved how the river never stopped moving, giving water to all who needed it, without ever asking for anything in return. Today, however, the river felt even more magical. Nanak sensed that it had a secret to share, a mystery hidden within its depths.

As Nanak wandered down the riverbank, his heart felt light. He had a strange urge to step closer to the water, to let the coolness of the river touch his feet. Without hesitation, he waded in, feeling the refreshing flow around him. He took a few more steps until he was waist-deep in the river, feeling as if the water itself was wrapping him in a gentle, invisible embrace.

Suddenly, a calm fell over him—a peace unlike anything he had ever felt before. It was as if the world had grown silent, and he could hear only the soft whispers of the river. His senses seemed to expand, and he felt connected to everything around him. The trees, the birds, the sky, the earth—everything felt alive and part of a single, beautiful whole. Nanak closed his eyes, letting himself drift into this feeling of unity, as if he were no longer a separate person but a part of something much greater.

When the sun rose higher in the sky, villagers began to go about their morning routines, but it didn't take long for someone to notice that Nanak was missing. His family grew worried; Nanak was usually the first to help with morning chores or ask his usual curious questions. Mata Tripta's heart beat faster with worry, and Mehta Kalu asked his neighbors if anyone had seen his son.

Word quickly spread through the village, and soon a small group had gathered to search for the young boy. They called out his name, searched the fields, and even looked in his favorite hiding places. But Nanak was nowhere to be found.

Mata Tripta tried to stay calm, but her worry grew with each passing moment. "Where could he have gone?" she whispered, looking toward the river with concern.

Some of the villagers began to search the riverbanks, fearing the worst. But as they drew near the water, they spotted a small, calm figure walking slowly toward them from the river's edge. It was Nanak, his face calm and radiant, as if he had just returned from a beautiful dream.

When Nanak reached the group, everyone noticed something different about him. His eyes seemed brighter, and his face glowed with a peacefulness that was almost magical. He smiled gently, as if he had discovered a wonderful secret and wanted to share it with the world.

Mata Tripta ran to her son and embraced him tightly. "Nanak! Where were you? We were so worried!"

Nanak looked up at his mother with a serene smile. "I was by the river, Mother," he said softly. "The river had something to show me."

The villagers gathered around, curious to hear what Nanak had to say. He had always been a thoughtful boy, but today he seemed different—as if he had glimpsed something beyond their understanding. Mehta Kalu, too, looked at his son with wonder, sensing that Nanak's heart was now filled with a wisdom beyond his years.

As the crowd settled around him, Nanak began to speak. His voice was calm, and he spoke with a clarity that surprised even the oldest villagers.

"Today, by the river, I felt something beautiful," he began. "I felt like I wasn't alone. I could feel the trees, the water, the birds, the sky... I felt them as if they were part of me."

The villagers listened, intrigued but puzzled. One of them asked, "What do you mean, Nanak? How can the trees or the river be a part of you?"

Nanak smiled, his eyes twinkling with kindness. "We are all connected," he explained. "Just like the river flows and nourishes the plants and animals without stopping to think of itself, we too are connected to each other, sharing the same life."

He paused, looking around at the faces of his friends and family. "Imagine if every person, every animal, and every plant was a part of one big family. Wouldn't we care for each other a little more? Wouldn't we share with those who have less? The river taught me that we don't need to hold on to things just for ourselves. We are all part of the same world, like leaves on the same tree."

The villagers were silent, lost in thought. Nanak's words were simple, yet they stirred something deep within each of them. Some looked down, feeling a sense of peace wash over them, while others wondered how such wisdom could come from a boy so young.

For the rest of the day, Nanak was lost in his own thoughts, reflecting on his experience by the river. He began to notice how everything around him was connected. When he watched a bird fly from one tree to another, he saw how it depended on the branches for rest. When he noticed the wind blowing through the fields, he saw how it carried the seeds that would grow into plants, feeding the animals and people alike.

As he walked through the village, Nanak's heart felt like it was overflowing with joy. He saw the world in a new way, as if each living thing was a friend, a part of himself. He began to feel a sense of gratitude for everything around him—the air he breathed, the sunlight that warmed him, the food he ate, and the people who loved him.

That night, as he lay down to sleep, Nanak whispered a quiet prayer of thanks, his heart filled with peace. He understood that life was not about keeping things for oneself but about sharing and connecting. It was a lesson that would stay with him forever and guide him on his journey.

In the days that followed, Nanak continued to share his simple message with those around him. When he saw someone in need, he reminded others to help them, saying, "We are all part of the same family." When he saw someone take more than they needed, he gently suggested, "Maybe we could leave some for others."

People in the village began to see things differently, inspired by Nanak's quiet wisdom. They realized that his words were not just lessons but a way of living that brought them closer together. His friends, too, were deeply moved by Nanak's message. They started to look at the world with fresh eyes, noticing the beauty in every small connection.

One evening, as the sun was setting, a stranger came to the village. He was a traveler from a distant land, tired and hungry from his journey. Nanak saw the man sitting by the side of the road, looking lost and weary. Without a second thought, he approached the stranger and offered him food and water.

The traveler accepted Nanak's kindness with gratitude, and they began to talk. "Why did you help me?" the stranger asked. "I am just a traveler, passing through. You don't even know me."

Nanak smiled warmly. "I helped you because we are all connected," he replied. "Just like the river flows to everyone, kindness should flow to all who need it. We are all part of the same world."

The traveler was touched by Nanak's words. He had met many people on his journey, but none had spoken with such sincerity and warmth. As he left the village, he carried Nanak's message with him, sharing it with others he met along the way.

As the chapter closes, young readers are invited to reflect on Nanak's discovery and imagine the beauty of feeling connected to everything around them. They are encouraged to notice the little connections in their own lives—between themselves and their friends, their families, their pets, and the world around them.

Through this magical experience by the river, children learn that kindness and compassion are not just acts—they are a way of living, a way of seeing the world as one big family. Nanak's realization becomes a gentle reminder that we, too, can find joy in connecting with others and in treating every person, plant, and animal as part of a beautiful whole.

Chapter 3: A Trade with Love

It was a bright, sunny day in Talwandi, and the fields were filled with golden crops swaying in the wind. Birds chirped from the trees, and farmers worked in the distance, tending to their fields. Nanak woke up that morning with a feeling of excitement, knowing that today would be different. Today, he would be taking his first steps into the world of trade.

His father, Mehta Kalu, was a respected figure in the village, known for his honesty and dedication to his work. He had often spoken to Nanak about the importance of working hard and earning a living. Today, Mehta Kalu had decided that his son was ready for his first task in business.

After breakfast, Mehta Kalu called Nanak to his side and handed him a small pouch of coins.

"Nanak, today I'm giving you an important responsibility," he began, his voice serious but gentle. "I want you to go to the neighboring village and buy some goods that we can sell here in Talwandi. This will help you understand the importance of trade and earning an honest livelihood."

Nanak listened carefully, nodding. Although he was excited, he couldn't help but feel that this task was more than just buying and selling goods. Deep in his heart, he sensed that there was a greater purpose to this day, something he couldn't quite put into words.

His father placed a firm but loving hand on Nanak's shoulder. "Remember, Nanak," he said, "use this money wisely and make sure you bring back something of value. I trust you to make the right choice."

With that, Nanak set off toward the neighboring village, the pouch of coins jingling softly as he walked. He carried his father's words in his heart, promising himself to make the most of this journey.

As Nanak walked along the dusty path, he took in the sights and sounds of the world around him. He passed farmers working in their fields, children playing in the open spaces, and merchants calling out to sell their goods in the marketplace. Everywhere he looked, he noticed how people were busy, each one working hard to earn a living and take care of their families.

After walking for a while, Nanak saw a small group of people gathered by the side of the road. They looked tired and weary, their clothes worn and dusty. Some of them were sitting on the ground, while others leaned against each other for support. It was clear to Nanak that these people were hungry and in need.

Nanak felt a tug at his heart. He knew his father had given him money to buy goods for trade, but he also knew that these people needed help. He paused, his mind racing. His father's words echoed in his mind: "Bring back something of value."

As he looked at the hungry faces before him, Nanak realized that sometimes, the most valuable thing we can give is not something we buy or sell—it is the kindness and compassion we show to others.

With a sense of purpose growing in his heart, Nanak made a decision. He approached the group and spoke gently, asking them about their journey and offering to help. They explained that they were travelers who had been walking for days without food, searching for work in nearby villages. Their voices were weak, and their faces bore the marks of exhaustion and hunger.

Nanak looked down at the pouch of coins in his hand and knew what he had to do. Instead of buying goods to sell, he would use the money to buy food for these people. He made his way to the nearest marketplace, where he bought bread, fruits, and water. With each purchase, he felt a deep sense of joy, knowing that this was the right choice.

When he returned to the travelers, he shared the food with them, watching as they ate gratefully. The sparkle in their eyes, the relief on their faces—it was a reward greater than any profit he could have made from selling goods. Nanak sat with them as they ate, listening to their stories, learning about their struggles and dreams. In that moment, he felt connected to them, as if they were all part of the same family.

After the travelers had eaten their fill, they thanked Nanak for his kindness and continued on their journey, their hearts filled with gratitude. Nanak watched them go, feeling a deep sense of peace. He knew he had done the right thing, even though he hadn't followed his father's instructions exactly.

With an empty pouch and a heart full of joy, Nanak began the journey back to Talwandi. Along the way, he reflected on the meaning of true wealth. It wasn't in coins or goods—it was in the love and kindness we share with others. He realized that helping those in need was a trade of the heart, a "Sacha Sauda," or true bargain, that brought happiness not only to others but also to oneself.

When Nanak reached home, Mehta Kalu was waiting for him. His father's face lit up when he saw his son, but his expression quickly turned serious as he noticed the empty pouch in Nanak's hands.

"Nanak, where are the goods?" his father asked, his voice filled with concern.

Nanak looked down, his gentle eyes meeting his father's. "I used the money to help some people who were hungry," he explained softly. "I saw them on my way to the village, and I felt that feeding them was the right thing to do."

Mehta Kalu's face clouded with disappointment. He had hoped that Nanak would learn the value of trade and the importance of making a living. "Nanak, I sent you to buy goods, not to give away our money," he said, his tone firm. "How will we support ourselves if we give everything away?"

Nanak listened respectfully to his father's words, understanding his concerns. But he also knew that he had made the right choice. He looked up at his father, his eyes shining with sincerity.

"Father," he said gently, "I felt that this was the best trade I could make. The joy in their eyes, the gratitude they showed—it was worth more than any goods I could have brought back. Sometimes, the greatest value lies in helping those who have nothing."

Mehta Kalu sighed, struggling to understand his son's choice. He knew that Nanak was kind-hearted and compassionate, but he also worried that such generosity could lead to hardship.

Just then, a wise elder from the village, who had overheard their conversation, stepped forward. He had known Nanak since he was a child and had seen the special light in him that set him apart.

"Mehta Kalu," the elder said, "your son has made a true bargain today. He has shared the wealth of his heart with those who needed it most. In doing so, he has brought more honor to your family than any trade could. His compassion will be remembered long after material goods are gone."

Mehta Kalu listened to the elder's words, his heart beginning to soften. He looked at his son, seeing not just a young boy, but a soul filled with wisdom beyond his years. Though he still worried about the future, he began to understand that Nanak's path was different, guided by a deep sense of love and compassion.

In the days that followed, Nanak continued to live by the values he held dear. He helped those in need, shared what he had, and showed kindness to everyone he met. The story of his "true bargain" spread throughout the village, inspiring others to look at kindness as a form of wealth.

People began to understand that generosity was not about what you gave, but how you gave it. By feeding the hungry and helping the less fortunate, Nanak showed that true wealth lay in service to others.

Nanak's father, too, began to see his son's actions in a new light. Though he had hoped Nanak would become a successful trader, he started to realize that his son was destined for something far greater. He saw that Nanak's heart was filled with love, a love that could not be measured in coins but was worth more than any wealth.

Chapter 4: Friends from All Paths

The sun was shining brightly over Talwandi as children ran through the fields, their laughter filling the air. Young Nanak was at the center of a group of children, his face lit up with excitement. It was the perfect day to spend with friends, and Nanak was eager to bring everyone together for a special game he had in mind.

Nanak looked around at his friends, who came from different families, beliefs, and backgrounds. There was Ayaan, the quiet boy from the neighboring village who came from a Muslim family; Meera, a spirited girl who loved to sing hymns in the temple; Hari, who helped his father tend the cows and often wore a tiny thread on his wrist as a sign of his Hindu faith; and there was also Tsering, who had recently arrived from a faraway land and brought stories of snow-covered mountains and prayer flags fluttering in the wind.

Each friend brought a unique story, a different way of seeing the world, and Nanak loved this diversity. He saw every friend as a colorful thread in a beautiful tapestry, each adding something special to the whole.

"Let's play a new game today!" Nanak announced, his eyes sparkling. The children gathered around, eager to hear his idea.

"What kind of game, Nanak?" Meera asked, her eyes wide with anticipation.

"It's called 'The Gift of My Path,'" Nanak explained. "In this game, each of us will share something special from our own traditions, beliefs, or family customs. It could be a story, a song, a favorite saying, or even something you bring from home."

The children looked at each other, intrigued. They loved Nanak's creative games and knew this one would be just as fun—and probably a little different, too.

"What's the prize?" Hari asked with a grin.

Nanak chuckled. "The prize is learning more about each other and seeing how beautiful our differences can be. By the end of the game, you'll see that each of our paths leads us to the same place."

The children nodded, some understanding Nanak's words, while others simply trusted that it would be a game worth playing. They each began to think of something special to share.

Ayaan was the first to step forward. He held a small prayer mat in his hands and looked shyly at his friends. "This is something my father taught me," he said. "It's a prayer that we say each day to remember God."

Ayaan laid out the mat on the ground, knelt down, and began to recite his prayer softly. The other children watched in silence, captivated by the gentleness of his voice and the sincerity in his eyes. They could feel the peace in his prayer, a sense of connection that went beyond words.

When Ayaan finished, Nanak clapped his hands softly, encouraging everyone else to do the same. "Thank you, Ayaan," he said warmly. "Your prayer teaches us the importance of humility and gratitude. It's a beautiful reminder to remember the One who created us."

The children nodded, feeling a quiet respect for Ayaan's prayer. They understood that even though they might pray differently, they all shared the same love for the divine.

Next, it was Meera's turn. She stepped forward with a wide grin and took a deep breath before launching into a song she had learned from her grandmother. It was a hymn, sung with a joyful voice, and it spoke of love and devotion.

The children were enchanted by Meera's song. Her voice soared, carrying words of praise and joy that lifted their spirits. As she sang, the other children could feel the happiness in her heart, as if her song were a bridge between them all.

When she finished, Nanak smiled at her. "Meera, your song reminds us that love and devotion are powerful gifts," he said. "Through your singing, you have shared your joy with all of us."

Meera beamed with pride, happy that her friends had enjoyed her song. She could see that even though her hymn was new to some of them, they felt the joy it carried, just as she did.

Hari was up next. He held out a small thread tied around his wrist, showing it to everyone. "In my family," he began, "we wear this thread to remember that we are all connected, like the sun and the stars."

He began to tell a story he had heard from his father. It was about a wise sage who had taught that all living beings were like rays from the same sun. Though they appeared separate, they were all part of one light, one family.

As he told the story, the children listened intently, imagining themselves as tiny stars, all part of a vast sky. Nanak nodded thoughtfully, feeling the truth in Hari's words.

"Hari, your story reminds us that we are all connected, no matter how different we seem," Nanak said. "It shows us that we are all part of the same light, sharing the same sky."

Hari smiled, happy to see his story bringing his friends closer together. Even those who hadn't heard the story before felt its warmth.

Tsering stepped forward with a handful of colorful cloths tied to strings. "These are called prayer flags," he explained. "In my home, we tie these flags on the mountaintops, and as the wind blows, the prayers are carried all around, blessing everyone."

He held up the flags, each one a different color, each one carrying a small message of peace, love, and kindness. The children touched the flags gently, feeling the softness of the cloth and imagining the prayers floating in the wind.

Nanak looked at the flags thoughtfully. "Tsering, these flags teach us that our wishes for peace and kindness can be shared with everyone, even if they are far away. It's a reminder that love knows no boundaries."

The children nodded, enchanted by the idea that a prayer could travel through the air like a gentle breeze, touching the hearts of people near and far.

As each child shared their story, the group grew closer, learning to appreciate the unique beauty in each of their traditions. Nanak felt his heart swell with joy, knowing that his friends were beginning to understand what he had felt all along—that true friendship didn't depend on following the same path. Instead, it thrived on understanding, respect, and a shared love for the divine in each of them.

Nanak gathered everyone together in a circle, inviting them to reflect on what they had learned from each other. He spoke softly, his voice filled with warmth.

"Today, we've shared our gifts with each other. Each of us follows a different path, but all our paths lead to the same place. The beauty of friendship is that it grows stronger with understanding and respect. No matter where we come from, we can be friends, just like we are today."

The children nodded, feeling a deep sense of connection. They realized that their differences didn't divide them—instead, they made their friendship richer and more vibrant.

To celebrate their newfound understanding, Nanak suggested one more game. He asked each child to pick a small stone from the ground, something unique to represent themselves. Then, they all placed their stones together in a small circle, creating a mosaic of different colors, shapes, and sizes.

"This circle of stones is like our friendship," Nanak explained. "Each stone is different, but together, they create something beautiful. Our friendship is like that too. When we respect each other's paths and learn from each other, we create something strong and beautiful."

The children gazed at the circle of stones, feeling proud of their unique contributions. They understood that just as each stone added something special to the circle, each friend brought something valuable to their friendship.

In the days that followed, the children continued to play together, their friendship strengthened by the understanding they had gained. They no longer saw their differences as barriers; instead, they saw them as gifts, pieces of a beautiful puzzle that fit together perfectly.

Nanak's message spread throughout the village, inspiring others to look at each person as a friend, regardless of their beliefs or background. People began to see that the true path of love and friendship was one that welcomed everyone, just as Nanak had shown.

For Nanak, this chapter in his life was a reminder that his journey would be guided by love, understanding, and acceptance. His friendships with children from different paths were like seeds, planted in the fertile soil of respect, ready to grow into a garden of unity.

Chapter 5: The Smallest Bow

It was a bright morning, and the journey had brought Nanak and his close friend, Mardana, to a new village. The villagers here were known for their wealth and high social standing, often looking down upon travelers who didn't seem wealthy or important. As Nanak and Mardana entered the village, they sensed the stares of people around them. Some murmured among themselves, casting glances that suggested judgment, while others walked past them without a word.

Mardana, noticing the villagers' coldness, felt uneasy. "They don't seem very welcoming, do they, Nanak?" he whispered. Mardana was accustomed to Nanak's calm, gentle presence, and he knew his friend was always treated with kindness and respect. But here, the air felt different, as if the villagers had already decided that Nanak and Mardana were not worth their time.

Nanak only smiled, his eyes calm as ever. "Remember, Mardana, each person carries their own pride and beliefs. It is our task to meet them with kindness."

As they walked through the village, they passed groups of villagers standing in front of their well-kept houses, their chests puffed with pride. One group of men, finely dressed in robes of rich colors, noticed the travelers and smirked.

"Look at those wanderers," one man said with a chuckle. "They seem to think they can just stroll through our village as if they belong here."

Another man added, "They're clearly not of our status. Look at their simple clothing and dusty feet!"

Nanak and Mardana heard their words but did not react. Mardana felt anger bubbling inside him, but Nanak's calm demeanor reminded him to stay composed. Nanak continued walking, looking straight ahead with quiet dignity, his expression unbothered by the villagers' remarks.

Soon, they reached the village square, where many of the prominent villagers had gathered. Among them was the village leader, Rajan, a tall man with a proud face. He was known for his wealth and influence, and his robes were embroidered with gold threads that gleamed in the sunlight. Rajan looked at Nanak and Mardana with disdain.

"Who are you strangers, and what brings you to our village?" he asked, his voice filled with pride.

Nanak bowed his head respectfully and answered, "We are merely travelers, here to see your village and to learn from the people we meet."

Rajan raised an eyebrow, unimpressed. "Learn from us? And what, exactly, could a simple traveler like you hope to learn from people of our standing?"

Nanak remained calm, his voice gentle as he replied, "Every person we meet teaches us something valuable. I hope to learn the importance of humility and kindness, qualities that we all can practice, regardless of our position."

Rajan and the others laughed at this, mistaking Nanak's humility for weakness. "Humility? That is the talk of simple men who have nothing to boast about," Rajan sneered. "We, on the other hand, have earned our pride."

Mardana felt his fists clench, his heart pounding with frustration. He didn't understand how Nanak could remain so peaceful in the face of such arrogance. Nanak, sensing Mardana's unease, placed a gentle hand on his shoulder, calming him. Then, Nanak did something that shocked everyone around him.

Without a word, Nanak bent down and gave a small, respectful bow to Rajan. His gesture was full of sincerity and peace, as if he were bowing not only to Rajan but to the spirit within him.

The crowd fell silent, watching this unexpected act. They were not used to seeing someone of such calm strength bowing before them, especially someone who looked so humble and ordinary. Nanak's small bow stirred something deep within them, something they had long buried under layers of pride.

Rajan was taken aback, unsure how to react. His proud posture wavered as he looked down at Nanak, who remained bowed for a moment before standing up with a peaceful smile. Nanak's gentle eyes held no resentment, only kindness.

"Why do you bow to me, traveler?" Rajan asked, his voice softer now, with a hint of curiosity.

Nanak replied, "I bow to the light within every person I meet, whether they show me kindness or not. Each soul deserves respect and love, and a bow is the simplest way to offer it."

Rajan's face flushed with confusion, for he had never encountered someone who would offer respect without expecting anything in return. He was accustomed to people bowing before him because of his wealth and power, but this felt different—like an invitation to see himself in a new way.

The villagers, who had been so eager to mock the travelers, now stood in silence. They, too, were affected by Nanak's humility and the way he had treated their leader with such grace. They began to question their own behavior and pride, wondering if they, too, could embrace such humility.

One of the villagers, a woman named Asha, stepped forward, her face softened by Nanak's example. "Forgive us, traveler," she said quietly.

"We are not used to seeing someone like you. We thought that pride was a sign of strength."

Nanak smiled kindly at her. "True strength is found not in pride, but in humility. When we let go of pride, we make room for kindness and love. It is like clearing a path through a forest. Only then can the light shine through."

Asha nodded, her heart touched by his words. She looked at the others, seeing the shift in their expressions. Slowly, the villagers' pride began to dissolve, replaced by a feeling they hadn't known before—a sense of respect for someone who, despite their unkindness, had treated them with grace.

After a moment, Nanak continued, "Imagine that we are all drops in the same river. If one drop boasts of its importance, it forgets that it is only part of a larger whole. By staying humble, we remember that we are all connected, and that our purpose is to flow together in harmony."

The villagers were moved by this simple, profound analogy. They had never thought of themselves as part of a larger whole; they had always focused on their own achievements, their own wealth, and their own pride. But Nanak's words opened their minds to the beauty of unity and humility.

Rajan, feeling the shift in the villagers around him, looked at Nanak with a newfound respect. "You have shown us something today that no wealth or status could teach," he admitted, his voice tinged with humility. "Perhaps we have been mistaken in our pride. Thank you for reminding us of the true strength that lies in kindness."

As Nanak and Mardana continued on their journey, the villagers watched them go, their hearts changed by the encounter. Rajan, who had once looked down on the travelers, felt a strange sense of peace.

He realized that Nanak's humility was not a sign of weakness, but a strength that was far greater than any wealth or power he could possess.

From that day on, the villagers began to see themselves in a new light. They started to treat each other with more kindness and respect, remembering Nanak's lesson that true strength comes from humility. They found joy in serving one another, and their village became a place where love and respect flourished.

Nanak's journey continues, but his example leaves a lasting impact on the village, reminding everyone—young and old—that humility is a gift we can give to ourselves and others.

Chapter 6: The Honest Hands

It was a warm morning in the village, and young Nanak could be found as he often was: near his family's fields, where the crops stood tall and green under the sunlight. The air was filled with the smell of earth, and every leaf seemed to glisten with the morning dew. Today was special, for Nanak had volunteered to help his family with their chores, and he was eager to contribute.

With a heart full of excitement, Nanak pulled on his work clothes and walked toward the fields where his father and the other villagers were busy. Though he was still young, his gentle spirit and eagerness to help had always impressed those around him. But today, he would learn that true joy was not just in working, but in doing so with honesty and love.

As Nanak arrived at the field, his father, Mehta Kalu, looked at him with a mixture of pride and concern. He knew that farming was hard work, and Nanak, being curious and sensitive, often found meaning in small things that others overlooked.

"Nanak," his father began, "the work here can be tiring, but it's what keeps food on our table. Are you sure you're ready for it?"

Nanak nodded with a warm smile. "Father, I want to help, and I want to feel the joy of working with my own hands."

Mehta Kalu handed him a small hoe and pointed to a row of crops. "Very well, then. Start here. Just remember, Nanak, an honest day's work is always worth more than anything gained without effort."

Nanak took the hoe and began to work, feeling a sense of satisfaction in each movement. He dug into the earth, feeling the soil slip through his fingers. Every clump of dirt he moved, every seed he touched felt like he was connecting with something greater than himself. His father watched him with a gentle smile, proud of his son's dedication.

As the hours went by, the sun climbed higher, and the work became harder. Nanak's arms began to tire, and the thought of taking a shortcut briefly crossed his mind. He glanced around and noticed that some other children, who were supposed to be working, had drifted off to play by the riverbank nearby.

A boy named Arjun noticed Nanak's hesitance and called out, "Come, Nanak! Leave the work for now. No one will notice if you take a break. Besides, we're just kids!"

Nanak felt the temptation to join his friends, to leave his tiring task behind and enjoy the cool water. But his heart reminded him of his father's words and of the promise he had made to himself. He took a deep breath and smiled at Arjun. "Thank you, my friend, but I want to finish this work. It brings me joy to know that I'm helping my family."

Arjun shrugged and ran off to join the others, while Nanak stayed behind, determined to complete his task with honesty. As he worked, he thought about how every small effort he put in would contribute to something bigger. He didn't need anyone watching over him to make him work hard—his own heart was his guide.

Later in the day, a wandering traveler named Bhai Lalo, known for his wisdom and his own dedication to honest work, came to the village. Hearing about Nanak's determination to help his family, he decided to pay him a visit. As Bhai Lalo approached, he saw the young boy diligently working under the hot sun, his face filled with both exhaustion and satisfaction.

Bhai Lalo watched for a moment, impressed by Nanak's dedication. "Young boy," he called out, "I have heard of your love for learning and your gentle heart. May I ask, what keeps you so committed to this work?"

Nanak looked up, wiping the sweat from his forehead, and smiled at the visitor. "I want to understand what it means to work honestly, Bhai Lalo. My father has always told me that there is pride in honest work, and I want to feel that for myself."

Bhai Lalo nodded approvingly. "Your father is wise. Honest work is like planting a seed—when done with sincerity, it grows into something beautiful, something that can nourish not just our bodies, but also our souls."

Nanak listened intently, taking Bhai Lalo's words to heart. "Then I will continue to work with my whole heart, for I want to plant seeds of honesty in all that I do."

That evening, as Nanak and his father returned home, a wealthy merchant arrived in the village, looking for workers to help carry his goods. The merchant was offering a higher wage for a shorter amount of work. Many villagers eagerly volunteered, tempted by the quick money, but they knew that the merchant often paid his workers only a fraction of what he promised.

Nanak's father looked at him thoughtfully. "The merchant's work may seem easier, Nanak, but remember that not all rewards are as they appear. Sometimes, the true reward lies in working for something we believe in, even if it doesn't pay as much."

Nanak pondered his father's words and decided to remain committed to his own family's work. Watching the other villagers rush to the merchant, he felt a small pang of doubt but remembered the sense of joy and satisfaction he had felt in working honestly in his family's field. He trusted that this path, though quieter, would bring him a greater peace.

The following morning, Nanak returned to the fields, feeling lighter than before. The work felt more meaningful, as if every seed he planted, every weed he pulled, was a small offering of love to his family and his village. He realized that when he worked with honesty, he felt connected to something larger than himself. The satisfaction he felt was deep and unshakable, unlike the fleeting excitement of quick rewards.

As he worked, a small group of children gathered nearby, watching Nanak in silence. They had heard about his choice to work honestly for his family, and they were moved by his dedication. One of the younger children, curious and inspired, asked, "Nanak, why do you work so hard when you could earn more doing something easier?"

Nanak paused and looked at the children with kindness. "It's not just about the reward, but about how the work makes me feel inside. When I work with honesty and love, it feels like I'm planting seeds of joy and peace that will grow within me."

The children were fascinated by this idea, and some even decided to stay and help Nanak, eager to experience the joy of honest work themselves.

As days turned into weeks, Nanak's dedication began to inspire the whole village. Slowly, the villagers began to see the value in working with integrity. They noticed how Nanak's fields flourished, the crops standing tall and vibrant. His work seemed blessed with a special kind of beauty, and they began to wonder if his honest approach was the reason.

Even the villagers who had worked for the wealthy merchant returned, realizing that the easy money they earned felt empty and unfulfilling. Watching Nanak, they started to help their families with renewed commitment, learning to find joy in their everyday tasks.

The village began to change, with each person contributing honestly to the work around them. The fields grew greener, the animals seemed happier, and the village became a place of harmony and prosperity. Children learned to help their parents with chores, and adults shared stories of how Nanak's example had taught them to work with integrity and love.

Through Nanak's dedication, children learn that every act, however small, can become a gesture of love when done with honesty. Nanak's humble hands, working in the soil, show them that the real treasure lies not in wealth, but in the joy that comes from honest efforts and a caring heart.

Chapter 7: Treasures of the Heart

The day dawned bright and clear as Nanak set off on a quiet path, walking through fields and villages where people went about their morning tasks. The air was filled with the sounds of birds chirping, and the cool breeze carried the fresh scent of blooming flowers. Today felt special, as though something important was waiting to unfold. As he walked, he noticed people busy in their lives—some with their families, others working hard in the fields or markets.

Soon, he came to a bustling village marketplace, where a large crowd had gathered around a grand cart adorned with bright, glittering jewels and luxurious silks. People whispered and pointed, admiring the cart and the man standing beside it, a wealthy merchant known as Malik Chand. Malik Chand was famous in the village for his great wealth, and he loved to show it off, often boasting about his riches to anyone who would listen.

Nanak watched the scene from a distance, intrigued not by the treasures on display but by the curious expressions of the people who surrounded the merchant. Their eyes were wide with awe as they admired the glimmering jewels and fine fabrics. However, Nanak's gaze shifted from Malik Chand to a humble figure nearby: an elderly farmer, dressed in simple, worn clothes, watching the scene with a soft smile. His gentle face showed no envy, only a peaceful contentment.

Malik Chand, noticing Nanak in the crowd, called out to him. "Young man!" he said, waving him over. "Come, see what true wealth looks like!"

The merchant opened a small chest lined with silk, revealing gold coins, silver ornaments, and sparkling gems. The crowd gasped, drawn to the sight of so much wealth, and murmured in admiration.

"This," Malik Chand declared, holding up a gold coin, "is the mark of a successful man! With wealth like mine, one can buy anything, from fine clothes to the best food. Tell me, young man, have you ever seen treasures like these?"

Nanak listened patiently, his gentle gaze resting on the merchant. "Yes, Malik Chand, you have many fine things, and they are certainly beautiful," he replied calmly. "But I wonder, what do you do with such wealth? Do you share it with others?"

The merchant chuckled, as though the question amused him. "Share it? Why would I do that? I have worked hard for my riches, and they belong to me. Only a fool would give away what he has earned."

Nanak smiled, not with judgment, but with compassion. "I see," he said softly, "yet, there are many kinds of wealth. Some treasures cannot be bought with gold or silver."

Malik Chand laughed heartily, thinking that Nanak's words were merely the thoughts of a simple village boy who could not understand the value of riches.

At that moment, the elderly farmer Nanak had noticed earlier approached them. He had watched the entire exchange between Nanak and Malik Chand, and his heart felt touched by the young boy's calm and thoughtful response. In his hand, the farmer held a single, ripe mango, the only piece of fruit he had harvested that day.

With a humble bow, the farmer extended the mango toward Nanak. "Young man," he said, his voice warm and sincere, "I don't have much, but please accept this mango as a token of my respect. You seem like a kind soul, and it would bring me joy to share what little I have with you."

Nanak accepted the mango with gratitude, holding it carefully in his hands as though it were the most precious gift. "Thank you," he said to the farmer, his eyes filled with appreciation. "This is truly a priceless gift, for it comes from a heart filled with love."

Malik Chand, watching this interaction, was puzzled. He looked at the simple mango in Nanak's hands, unable to understand how anyone could value a plain piece of fruit over glittering jewels and gold.

Sensing Malik Chand's confusion, Nanak turned to him with a gentle smile. "Malik Chand, do you see the difference between the treasures in your chest and this mango?"

The merchant shook his head, frowning. "I don't understand. How could a single mango possibly be worth more than gold?"

"True wealth is not measured by how much we possess," Nanak explained, "but by the love and generosity in our hearts. This mango, though simple, is filled with the farmer's kindness and a spirit of sharing. He has given what he has, not because he has much, but because he has a generous heart."

Malik Chand looked at the farmer, who stood quietly, his eyes reflecting the joy of giving. The merchant felt a pang of realization, something he hadn't felt before—a sense that perhaps his riches lacked something essential, something that couldn't be bought.

Nanak continued, "Wealth gained for oneself alone can bring little happiness. But when we give from our hearts, no matter how little, it becomes a treasure for both the giver and the receiver."

Malik Chand pondered Nanak's words. His life had been dedicated to gathering riches, yet he realized that he had rarely found the true happiness he sought. The admiration of the crowd, the sparkle of his jewels—all seemed fleeting compared to the genuine joy on the farmer's face as he shared his only mango with Nanak.

Humbled, Malik Chand approached the farmer. "My friend," he said softly, "I have far more wealth than you, yet I have never given so freely as you have today. You have shown me that true richness lies not in keeping, but in sharing."

With a newfound understanding, Malik Chand reached into his chest and pulled out several coins. He handed them to the farmer, who looked at him in surprise. "Please, accept this as a token of my respect. I want to learn what it means to be generous, like you."

The farmer accepted the coins with gratitude, but more than the gift itself, he cherished the merchant's change of heart. Nanak smiled, seeing how even a small act of kindness could create a ripple of change, transforming hearts and opening eyes to a deeper truth.

As the day went on, the villagers who had gathered in the marketplace talked about what they had seen. Some were inspired by Malik Chand's decision to give, while others marveled at the kindness of the farmer who had shared his only fruit. Nanak's gentle wisdom had shown them all that wealth is not defined by how much one has, but by how much one gives.

From that day, Malik Chand began sharing his wealth with those in need, finding joy in helping others. The farmer, too, continued to share his simple meals and humble possessions, feeling a deeper sense of happiness and fulfillment.

Nanak's words stayed with everyone, a reminder that true treasures are not found in gold or jewels, but in the love and generosity that flow from an open heart.

Chapter 8: The Melodies of Love

It was a calm evening in the village. The sun had begun to set, casting a warm, golden glow over the fields and rivers. Birds chirped as they returned to their nests, and a soft breeze rustled through the trees. People were finishing their work for the day, preparing for a restful evening with their families. However, the villagers noticed something unusual—a faint sound drifting through the air, unlike anything they had heard before. It was a soft, gentle melody, carrying with it a sense of peace and warmth.

Curious, the villagers followed the sound, tracing it to an open field just beyond the village. There, sitting under a large tree, they found Nanak with his friend, Mardana. Mardana was holding a small instrument, a rabab, gently plucking the strings while Nanak sang in a soft, soothing voice. His words were simple yet filled with a love that seemed to embrace everyone who heard them.

The villagers gathered around, some sitting on the grass, others standing quietly. They listened, enchanted by the beauty of the song. Nanak's voice rose and fell like a gentle breeze, reaching each listener's heart, bringing with it a calmness that washed away the worries of the day. The children, too, sat in wonder, captivated by the music's magic.

As the song ended, Nanak looked at the villagers, his face radiant with joy. "Music," he began, "is a language that speaks to our hearts. It is a gift we all can share, a way to bring joy to others without needing any words."

A young boy in the crowd raised his hand, his eyes wide with wonder. "Nanak ji," he asked, "how can music make us feel so happy, even without saying anything?"

Nanak smiled, his gaze warm and kind. "Music carries the love within our hearts," he explained. "When we sing with kindness and joy, others can feel it too. Music connects us all, reminding us that we are never alone, that we are all part of one beautiful melody."

The children nodded, trying to understand this idea. They had always thought of music as just sounds or songs, but Nanak's words showed them a new way to think about it—as a language of love that anyone could understand, no matter where they were from or what they believed.

Nanak and Mardana invited everyone to join them in singing. "Come, sing with us," Nanak encouraged, gesturing for the villagers to sit closer. "Let's fill this evening with our voices, and let the world hear the melody of our hearts."

The villagers hesitated at first, feeling a bit shy, but Nanak's warm smile put them at ease. Slowly, one by one, they began to hum along, and soon their voices rose together, blending into a gentle chorus. The children, too, joined in, their young voices bright and lively, adding a joyful energy to the gathering.

As they sang, something magical happened—the villagers could feel their spirits lifting, their worries melting away. The music brought them closer together, filling their hearts with happiness and a sense of belonging. It didn't matter that some were farmers, others merchants, and some travelers passing through; in that moment, they were all one, united by the love in their voices.

Nanak looked around, his heart filled with gratitude. This was the power of music—a force that could heal, uplift, and connect. He saw the smiles on the villagers' faces, the way they looked at one another with kindness, and he knew that this simple act of singing together had made a difference.

As the night deepened, Nanak began to sing a new song, one with a gentle, steady rhythm. In this song, he sang about the beauty of kindness, the strength of compassion, and the joy of unity. His words were like a warm embrace, carrying messages of love and peace that everyone could understand.

He sang about how we are all part of the same world, how each of us has a light within us that shines brightly when we are kind and loving. He reminded them that, just as different notes come together to create a beautiful melody, so do people from different walks of life come together to create a harmonious world.

"Think of each person as a note in a song," Nanak said, pausing between verses. "If we each sing our note with love, we create a melody that is beautiful and whole. But if we are harsh or unkind, the song becomes difficult to listen to. So let us each do our part to create a melody of peace, one that brings joy to all who hear it."

The villagers nodded, deeply moved by Nanak's words. His song had shown them that love and kindness were not only values to hold in their hearts but also melodies to share with others, creating harmony in the world.

As the villagers continued to sing, a group of travelers approached, drawn by the sound of music. These travelers were from a distant village and had stopped for the night nearby. They had never met Nanak or the villagers, but the music welcomed them, inviting them to join.

Seeing the new faces, Nanak and Mardana welcomed them with open arms. "Please, join us," Nanak said warmly. "This music is for everyone, a gift to be shared."

The travelers were surprised, as they had expected to be met with hesitation or suspicion, being strangers. But Nanak's kindness and the warmth of the villagers made them feel at home. They joined in the singing, feeling the same peace and joy that had touched the others.

Through music, the villagers and the travelers became friends, sharing smiles and laughter, their differences forgotten. In that moment, they were united, not by words or promises but by the simple joy of singing together.

As the evening came to a close, Nanak shared one final thought. "Let us remember that music, like love, has no boundaries. It belongs to everyone, and it can bring us together no matter where we come from or who we are. When we sing with love, we create a world that is more peaceful, more joyful."

He encouraged the villagers and travelers to carry this message with them, to share music with others wherever they went. "Let your hearts be filled with melodies of kindness and love," he said, "and let them echo in the world around you."

The villagers and travelers left that evening with full hearts, each carrying a piece of the music in their souls. Nanak's words stayed with them, a reminder that love and kindness could be shared without words, through the simple, beautiful act of singing together.

Chapter 9: The Kind Heart Challenge

It was a bright morning in the village. Nanak and his friends were gathered under a big tree, where they often met to talk and play games. Today, however, they noticed that Nanak seemed especially excited about something. His eyes sparkled, and he wore a playful smile that made everyone curious.

One of his friends, Amrit, couldn't hold back and asked, "Nanak, you seem extra happy today! What's on your mind?"

Nanak grinned and replied, "I have a challenge for all of you. But it's not just any challenge—it's a 'kind heart' challenge."

The children exchanged curious glances. They had played many games together, from hide-and-seek to racing across the fields, but they had never heard of a "kind heart" challenge before.

"What's a 'kind heart' challenge?" asked Leela, a little girl with a big, adventurous spirit.

Nanak explained, "The 'kind heart' challenge is about finding small ways to make people happy and to help them throughout the day. Imagine how wonderful it would be if each of us did five acts of kindness today. The whole village would be filled with smiles!"

The children's faces lit up at the idea. The thought of spreading happiness in their village filled them with excitement. They loved playing games with Nanak, but this was something different, something that felt special.

Nanak continued, "Here are the rules. Each of us has to find five ways to be kind today. It can be as simple as helping someone carry something, sharing our food, or even giving a smile to someone who looks sad. But it must come from the heart."

He paused, letting the idea sink in. "At the end of the day, we'll come back here under this tree and share what we did. I can't wait to hear all the wonderful things you'll do!"

The children clapped their hands in excitement, and each of them began thinking of different ways they could spread kindness. They were all determined to rise to Nanak's challenge and make their village a happier place.

Amrit decided to start right away. As they left the tree, he saw an elderly woman walking slowly along the road, carrying a heavy bundle of firewood. She looked tired, and Amrit's heart went out to her. Without hesitating, he ran over to her and offered, "May I help you carry that?"

The woman looked surprised at first, but then a grateful smile spread across her face. "Oh, thank you, dear boy! My old bones aren't as strong as they used to be."

Amrit took the bundle and walked alongside her, chatting and listening as she told him stories of the village from many years ago. When they reached her home, she patted his head kindly and thanked him again. Amrit felt a warm glow inside. It was such a small thing, but it felt wonderful to help someone.

Leela, meanwhile, had thought of another way to spread kindness. During lunch, she saw her friend Charan sitting alone, looking a bit down. She walked over to him and offered, "Would you like to share my snacks? My mother made my favorite treats today!"

Charan looked up and smiled, a little shyly. "Thank you, Leela," he said, accepting her offer. They sat together, munching on treats and chatting about their day. Charan's face brightened, and Leela was happy to see him smiling again. Sharing her food had brought them both joy, and she realized how a small act could change someone's entire day.

Another child, Ravi, noticed that his teacher, Master Singh, often had a dry throat from talking all day. Ravi thought it would be a kind gesture to bring him a cup of cool water between lessons.

During the break, he filled a small cup from the well and quietly placed it on his teacher's desk. Master Singh looked up in surprise and smiled warmly. "Thank you, Ravi," he said. "That was very thoughtful of you."

Ravi felt proud and happy. He hadn't needed to do anything big—just a simple gesture to show care and respect. But Master Singh's appreciative smile was reward enough.

As the day went on, Nanak was also busy with his own acts of kindness. While walking through the village, he noticed two boys arguing over a game. Their voices were loud, and both looked upset. Instead of walking away, Nanak gently approached them.

"What's the matter?" he asked, his voice calm and friendly.

The boys explained their disagreement, each convinced he was right. Nanak listened patiently to both sides, nodding thoughtfully. Then, with a smile, he offered a simple suggestion: "What if you each take turns? That way, you both get to play and enjoy the game."

The boys considered his advice and eventually agreed. They realized that sharing was more fun than arguing, and they thanked Nanak for helping them find a solution. Nanak walked away, knowing that sometimes, kindness is just being willing to listen and offer a gentle word.

As Leela continued her "kind heart" challenge, she noticed a stray dog looking hungry and lonely near the village entrance. She had a piece of bread with her that she had saved for later, but seeing the dog, she decided that he needed it more.

She approached the dog slowly and gently, extending her hand with the bread. The dog's tail began to wag, and he looked up at her with grateful eyes. Leela felt a rush of happiness as the dog ate the bread, wagging his tail even faster. It was a small act, but it made her feel connected to the world around her in a special way.

As the sun began to set, the children gathered back under the big tree where they had started their day. Each of them was eager to share what they had done and hear about each other's acts of kindness.

Amrit went first, proudly describing how he had helped the elderly woman with her bundle of firewood. His friends listened with admiration, nodding as he explained how happy she had been.

Next, Leela shared her story of sharing snacks with Charan and feeding the stray dog. Her friends smiled, understanding how those small gestures could mean so much.

Ravi recounted his water gesture for Master Singh, and they all agreed it was a thoughtful way to show kindness. Then, it was Nanak's turn. He told them about how he had helped the two boys resolve their argument, showing that sometimes kindness meant helping others find peace.

Each child had found unique and creative ways to spread kindness, and they were thrilled by the happiness they had brought to others. They realized that kindness didn't have to be a grand act—small gestures, like offering a smile, helping someone carry something, or sharing a snack, could make a big difference.

Nanak looked around at his friends, his heart filled with pride and joy. "You have all done wonderfully today," he said. "Kindness is like a seed. When we plant it in the hearts of others, it grows and spreads, creating a world filled with love and happiness."

The children nodded, understanding that their kindness was not just a one-time challenge but a way of life. Inspired by Nanak's words, they decided to make the "kind heart" challenge a regular game.

Every day, they would try to find small ways to be kind, spreading joy throughout the village.

The "Kind Heart Challenge" teaches us that kindness can be simple, fun, and something they can do every day. By finding small ways to help others, they can make a big difference in the world around them.

Chapter 10: The Lion's Roar of Truth

The sun was shining brightly over the village, casting a warm glow over the fields and pathways. Nanak was on his way to the village square with his friends, where a group of villagers had gathered. It was market day, and people were busy buying and selling goods. The air was filled with the sounds of haggling, laughter, and the occasional clink of coins.

As they strolled through the square, Nanak's eyes fell on a commotion near one of the stalls. A wealthy merchant, who often traded in spices and textiles, stood in the middle of a small crowd, loudly accusing a poor farmer of trying to cheat him. The farmer, who was visibly distressed, was clutching a small basket of fruits, his hands trembling as he tried to defend himself.

Nanak's friends noticed the commotion too. Amrit, always curious, tugged at Nanak's sleeve. "Nanak, let's see what's going on!"

The children moved closer, eager to understand the situation. As they drew near, they could hear the merchant's booming voice.

"You think you can trick me with these rotten fruits?" the merchant accused, his eyes narrow with anger. "How dare you try to sell me such low-quality goods!"

The farmer, head bowed, spoke in a quiet, shaky voice. "Sir, I swear, these fruits are fresh. I picked them from my own orchard this morning."

The merchant scoffed, pointing a finger at the man. "Lies! You're just trying to make a quick coin off of me. I should take this matter to the village elders and have you punished!"

The farmer looked around, his face pale with fear. He clearly had no one to stand up for him, and the crowd seemed unsure, casting glances at one another without anyone daring to intervene.

Nanak's heart ached as he watched the scene unfold. The farmer was clearly distressed, and it was clear that the merchant's harsh words were causing him even more anxiety. Nanak could see that the farmer was a humble, honest man who likely depended on his small orchard to make a living.

Taking a deep breath, Nanak stepped forward. He wasn't sure what the outcome would be, but he knew he couldn't stand by and let this injustice continue.

With a calm but strong voice, Nanak spoke up. "Excuse me, sir. But perhaps there has been some misunderstanding here."

The merchant turned, surprised to see a young boy addressing him so directly. He sneered, "What business does a child have in matters of trade? Go along now, little one. This is no place for children."

But Nanak did not move. His voice was steady and respectful, yet filled with a quiet strength. "Respectfully, I believe this farmer speaks the truth. His fruits appear fresh and good. Maybe we can solve this without anger."

The merchant's face darkened. "How dare you question me? This man is trying to cheat me, and you defend him? What would you know about honesty?"

Nanak looked directly at the merchant, his eyes calm but unwavering. "I know that accusing someone without proof is unkind. And I know that truth is more powerful than wealth or status. If this man has done nothing wrong, then he deserves to be treated with respect."

The crowd murmured, impressed by Nanak's courage. It was rare for anyone to stand up to the merchant, who was known to be influential and well-connected. Yet here was a young boy, calmly defending a poor farmer with nothing but his words.

The merchant scoffed but found himself slightly unnerved by Nanak's presence. "You think you can prove that these fruits are fresh?" he challenged, crossing his arms.

Nanak nodded thoughtfully, then turned to the farmer. "May I have one of your fruits?" he asked kindly.

The farmer nodded, still looking unsure but grateful for Nanak's support. He handed Nanak a ripe apple from his basket, his hands still trembling. Nanak held the apple up for everyone to see.

"Let us all see for ourselves," Nanak suggested. He took a small bite of the apple and then smiled, holding up the bitten fruit for everyone to observe. "It's fresh and sweet," he said, his voice carrying over the crowd.

Some of the onlookers chuckled softly, while others nodded in agreement. They could see that the apple was indeed fresh, and Nanak's simple test had shown the merchant's accusation to be groundless.

The merchant shifted uncomfortably, realizing that the crowd was now watching him with a mix of skepticism and disapproval. He cleared his throat, looking slightly embarrassed.

"Well... perhaps I was too quick to judge," he muttered, unwilling to admit he was wrong. But the message was clear—Nanak's courage and calm truth had shifted the situation, exposing the merchant's unfair treatment.

Turning back to the farmer, Nanak placed a reassuring hand on his shoulder. "You have nothing to fear," he said kindly. "Truth has a way of making itself known, even when others try to hide it."

The farmer's eyes filled with gratitude. "Thank you, young master," he whispered, his voice choked with emotion. "I didn't know what I would have done without your help."

Nanak smiled, shaking his head. "No need to thank me. It was simply the right thing to do. We must all look out for each other, especially when someone is treated unfairly."

The crowd murmured in agreement, and some even began to disperse, satisfied that justice had been served. Nanak's friends watched in admiration, inspired by his courage to speak up for someone who couldn't defend himself.

Later that evening, as the sun dipped below the horizon, Nanak and his friends sat by the riverbank, reflecting on the events of the day. Amrit broke the silence, his voice filled with awe. "Nanak, I can't believe you stood up to the merchant like that. Weren't you afraid?"

Nanak smiled, gazing at the rippling water. "Fear can make us silent, but truth is stronger than fear. When we speak with honesty and kindness, even the biggest problems can be solved. It's like a lion's roar—powerful, yet calm. Truth doesn't need to shout or hurt others. It just needs to be heard."

Leela nodded, her face thoughtful. "I want to be brave like that too. I didn't know that standing up for someone could feel so powerful."

Nanak chuckled softly. "Courage is not always loud or fierce. Sometimes, it's as simple as saying, 'This isn't fair,' or 'I don't agree.' When we stand up for others, we help bring fairness and kindness to the world."

The "lion's roar" of truth that Nanak had demonstrated inspired not just his friends but also others in the village. Word of the incident quickly spread, and the villagers were moved by the courage of the young boy who had spoken up for justice.

Even the merchant, who had initially felt humiliated, found himself reflecting on his actions. The calm, fearless way that Nanak had addressed him had left a deep impression. Gradually, the merchant began to treat others with more respect, realizing that fairness and kindness could bring him far more peace than wealth ever could.

Chapter 11: A Circle of Equals

One bright morning, the villagers bustled about as they prepared for a special gathering by the riverbank. Word had spread that Nanak was planning to host a large meal, open to everyone in the village and beyond. Curious, people from different walks of life—farmers, merchants, travelers, and artisans—made their way to the gathering spot, wondering what this young boy might have to share.

Nanak's friends helped him set up rows of simple woven mats on the grassy ground, creating a large, open circle where everyone would soon sit together. Nanak's family, and even a few elders, looked on with a mix of curiosity and admiration, unsure what Nanak had planned but moved by the peaceful atmosphere he had created.

As people began to arrive, Nanak welcomed each of them with a warm smile and a gentle invitation. "Please, find a place anywhere in the circle," he said kindly. "There is room for everyone here."

One of the first to arrive was Bhagat, an elderly farmer who often felt overlooked by the wealthier villagers. He was surprised when Nanak greeted him with the same warmth he gave to everyone else, guiding him to sit wherever he liked.

Soon after, a merchant arrived, wearing fine clothes and carrying a pouch of coins. Used to his high status, the merchant looked around, searching for a seat that might honor his position. But he noticed that no seat seemed any better than another—each mat was as simple as the next, placed equally within the circle.

"Shouldn't the wealthy be seated separately?" the merchant asked Nanak, raising an eyebrow.

Nanak gently shook his head, smiling. "Here, we are all equal. This circle has no head and no tail; no one is higher or lower. When we share a meal, we also share the same spirit of love and respect."

The merchant, puzzled but moved by Nanak's words, took his place beside the elderly farmer. And as others arrived, they too settled down in the circle, finding themselves seated beside people from all different backgrounds. A shoemaker sat next to a teacher, a fruit seller beside a carpenter, all equal within the circle.

Once everyone was seated, Nanak walked around, greeting each guest and helping to serve them simple bowls of lentils, warm flatbread, and water. He made sure everyone had enough food and, in his calm and gentle way, invited the children to help him serve as well.

Amrit, who had always admired Nanak's kindness, carried a bowl of lentils to an elderly woman. Leela offered a plate of flatbread to a group of travelers. Together, the children experienced the joy of serving others and sensed the warm, friendly atmosphere that filled the gathering.

As everyone began to eat, Nanak took his own seat on the mat, joining the circle just like everyone else. His presence felt comforting, and his smile encouraged others to relax and enjoy the meal.

"Today, we are all here as friends," he said softly, his voice carrying a deep kindness. "No one is greater or lesser than anyone else. In this circle, each of us is part of a family."

As they ate, some of the children started to ask Nanak questions, curious about the meaning behind this unique gathering.

"Bhai Nanak," a young girl named Meera began, "why did you make us sit in a circle?"

Nanak took a sip of water, his eyes twinkling as he answered. "A circle has no beginning and no end. It's like the sun or the moon. When we sit in a circle, we are saying that no one here is above or below another. We are all equal, like parts of one big family."

Another child, Dev, raised his hand shyly. "But... aren't some people more important than others? Like, aren't the leaders of the village more special?"

Nanak smiled at Dev, appreciating his question. "Each person has a different role, just as each flower in a garden is unique. But every flower is beautiful in its own way. Just as a garden needs all kinds of flowers to be colorful, our community needs each person's unique gifts. A leader may guide, but he is no more special than the farmer who grows our food or the potter who makes our cups."

The children nodded, absorbing his words. They began to look around the circle, noticing the diversity of people gathered there. Some wore simple clothes, while others wore colorful fabrics; some were older, while others were young; some were quiet, while others whispered excitedly with their neighbors.

To help everyone understand the value of equality, Nanak began to tell a story as they ate. His voice was gentle, but the words held everyone's attention.

"Once upon a time," he started, "there was a great tree in the forest, tall and strong. It had large branches that gave shade to all who passed beneath it. The tree was proud of its strength and often boasted to the smaller plants and flowers around it."

Nanak paused, looking around the circle. "One day, a storm came, with fierce winds and heavy rain. The great tree tried to stand tall against the storm, but its branches were torn, and it began to fall."

The crowd listened in silence, drawn into the story. Nanak continued, "After the storm, the small plants, which had bent low to the ground, were unharmed. They were not proud like the great tree; they were humble and close to the earth. They survived because they accepted their place in the forest. The storm had taught the tree that every plant, big or small, has a purpose."

Looking into the eyes of those gathered around him, Nanak concluded, "And so, like the plants in the forest, each of us is valuable, no matter our size, strength, or wealth. Together, we make up the beauty and strength of our community."

As Nanak finished his story, a sense of understanding filled the circle. People from different backgrounds, who rarely interacted before, found themselves smiling and chatting with one another, realizing that they all shared the same simple joys and challenges in life.

The merchant, who had initially felt hesitant to sit among the villagers, softened. For the first time, he saw the value in people he had previously ignored, recognizing their kindness, hard work, and friendship.

Beside him, the elderly farmer looked up with a twinkle in his eye, feeling that for the first time, he was truly seen and respected, regardless of his humble status.

Nanak's teachings had created a beautiful harmony among everyone present. The circle of equals was no longer just a seating arrangement; it had become a symbol of unity and respect.

As the meal came to an end, Nanak invited everyone to join hands. "May we always remember that no one is too great or too small in the circle of life," he said, his voice filled with warmth. "When we respect one another, we grow stronger as a community."

With joined hands, the villagers looked around at one another, realizing that they were bound by more than just their presence at the meal—they were connected by a shared sense of belonging and respect.

Chapter 12: The Calm Stone

One day, as the sun rose above the village, the children gathered at their usual spot by the riverbank to wait for Nanak, eager for another story or lesson from their beloved friend and teacher. However, that morning felt different; a faint tension filled the air, and the children soon discovered the reason.

A group of villagers approached Nanak with a problem that had troubled them deeply. They explained that their crops were withering due to a lack of water. The river, their primary source for irrigation, had suddenly started flowing in a weaker trickle than usual. While it hadn't dried up completely, the reduced flow meant their crops were at risk.

"We don't know what to do, Nanak," one farmer said worriedly. "We've tried digging channels and clearing debris, but nothing seems to improve the flow. The village depends on this river."

The children listened attentively, sensing the worry in the adults' voices. They, too, were affected by the situation, as they knew the importance of the crops for the village's food supply. The farmers and children looked to Nanak with hope, anticipating that he would have a quick solution to the problem.

However, Nanak simply nodded, his face calm and thoughtful. He didn't rush to speak or offer advice. Instead, he walked slowly over to a large, flat stone near the riverbank, gesturing for the children to follow him.

"Let's sit for a while," he suggested, settling himself on the stone with a peaceful smile. "Sometimes, the answer comes when we take the time to listen and observe."

The children and villagers exchanged puzzled glances, unsure of what to make of Nanak's suggestion. But trusting his wisdom, they joined him, sitting quietly along the riverbank. The sound of the

gently flowing water filled the silence, and the cool breeze rustled through the trees, creating a soothing, almost magical atmosphere.

The children sat on the grass around Nanak, their curiosity growing as they watched him remain still, his eyes focused on the river. As time passed, they noticed his peaceful expression, as though he were in deep thought or simply enjoying the gentle flow of the water.

Finally, a boy named Aarav, known for his energetic and restless nature, couldn't hold back any longer. "Bhai Nanak, aren't we supposed to do something? Shouldn't we find a way to fix the river's flow?"

Nanak looked at Aarav with a gentle smile. "Sometimes, the best thing we can do is to become still, like this stone," he said, patting the large rock beside him. "Imagine if this stone moved each time the river changed. Would it ever be able to see what is truly happening?"

The children exchanged curious glances, intrigued by Nanak's words. They had never thought of calmness as a solution. To them, solving a problem always seemed to mean action—doing something, fixing something, or changing things immediately.

Nanak continued, "Imagine you are a stone resting by the river, watching everything around you. The water flows past, sometimes strong, sometimes slow. The animals come and go, and the weather changes from sunny to rainy. But as the stone, you remain calm, observing everything. In time, you start to see patterns. You understand the flow of the river, the path of the animals, and the dance of the seasons. Patience reveals the answers."

The children leaned forward, captivated by Nanak's story. His words painted a picture in their minds of a calm stone watching the world with silent wisdom. They imagined themselves as that stone, learning from the stillness and finding peace in the act of waiting.

The villagers, too, began to relax, their initial worry fading as they absorbed Nanak's message. They realized that perhaps their anxious rushing and attempts to control the river had prevented them from seeing a solution.

As they sat by the river, Nanak suddenly pointed to a spot further downstream where the water was blocked by a pile of branches and debris that had collected over time. The villagers gasped as they noticed it too. It was an area they hadn't thought to check, as it was farther from their usual irrigation channels.

Nanak rose, his eyes still calm and focused. "Sometimes, by becoming still and observing closely, we notice things we might have missed in our hurry. That pile of debris is affecting the flow of the water."

The farmers and children were amazed. In their rush to solve the problem, they had overlooked this simple cause. The children felt a sense of awe and respect for Nanak's patience and quiet wisdom. They realized that, by sitting calmly and observing, they had found the solution naturally.

The villagers quickly worked together to remove the debris, using sticks and tools to clear the blockage. Within minutes, the river's flow began to strengthen, and the water returned to its normal, nourishing course. The children cheered, their faces bright with happiness, as they watched the river flow freely once more.

As the villagers returned to their work, Nanak gathered the children around him again, sitting back on the stone that had become a silent teacher in its own right.

"Remember, children," Nanak said, his voice soft and steady, "just like the river, life sometimes flows smoothly, and other times it faces obstacles. But by becoming calm and patient, like this stone, we can learn to understand the flow and find solutions with a clear mind."

One of the children, Meera, spoke up thoughtfully. "So, when we have a problem, we should sit quietly and think instead of rushing to fix it right away?"

Nanak nodded, pleased by her understanding. "Yes, Meera. Patience allows us to see things as they are, without the confusion of worry or haste. Sometimes, answers come not from doing, but from simply being."

The children nodded, understanding the value of patience in a new light. They felt inspired to practice calmness in their own lives, just as Nanak had shown them by the river that day.

Inspired by Nanak's lesson, the children created a game called "The Calm Stone Challenge." They took turns trying to remain completely still and quiet, like the stone by the river, while the others gently tried to distract them. If someone managed to stay calm and unmoved for a whole minute, they earned the title of "Calm Stone Champion."

The game became a favorite pastime among the children, and they learned that practicing calmness was both fun and helpful. They found that the more they practiced, the easier it became to stay patient and think clearly during tricky situations.

Soon, the "Calm Stone Challenge" spread throughout the village, and even some of the adults joined in, finding joy and peace in the simple act of being still.

Chapter 13: The Gifts of Earth and Sky

One early morning, as the children gathered near Nanak's home, they noticed him preparing for what looked like an adventure. He was wrapping a small bundle of food and filling a flask with fresh water, his face bright with anticipation.

"Where are you going, Bhai Nanak?" asked a young girl named Chanda, her eyes wide with curiosity.

Nanak smiled. "Today, I thought we'd visit the forest," he replied. "The forest has many stories to tell, and if we listen carefully, it will share its secrets."

The children exchanged excited glances, eagerly following him along the path leading to the nearby woods. It was a place filled with the mystery of chirping birds, rustling leaves, and hidden trails, and they couldn't wait to see what Nanak would reveal to them.

As they ventured deeper into the forest, Nanak led them to a small clearing where the sunlight poured through the branches above, casting golden patches on the forest floor. He knelt down and pointed to a line of tiny ants marching diligently across a fallen leaf.

"Look at these little ants," he said softly. "They are small, yet they work together, each one carrying a piece of food. They live together, help each other, and form their own little world."

The children watched in awe as the ants moved in perfect formation, carrying bits of food much larger than themselves. The children marveled at how something so small could be so strong and organized.

"Why do they work so hard, Bhai Nanak?" asked a boy named Ravi, his face thoughtful.

Nanak replied, "They work not just for themselves, but for each other. They understand that their strength lies in unity. The forest has taught them that when each one plays their part, the whole group can thrive."

The children nodded, beginning to see the forest as a place of life and cooperation, where even the tiniest creatures contributed something important.

After watching the ants, Nanak led the children to an area filled with tall trees. He placed a hand gently on the trunk of an old, sturdy tree, his fingers tracing the bark as if greeting an old friend.

"These trees," he said, looking up at the towering branches, "they are guardians of this forest. They give us shade, shelter, and even the air we breathe. They stand tall and strong, yet they ask for nothing in return."

A little girl named Amrita placed her hand on the tree trunk, mimicking Nanak's gesture. "Do trees talk, Bhai Nanak?" she asked in a whisper, as if not wanting to disturb the tree.

Nanak chuckled gently. "Yes, they do, but not with words. The trees speak with their leaves, their branches, and their roots. They communicate through their silence, teaching us the value of patience and resilience."

He pointed out the branches stretching towards the sky, leaves dancing softly in the breeze. "They remind us to stand firm yet reach for the sky. And like us, they have families—other trees, plants, and creatures who live around them."

The children took a moment to close their eyes and listen, tuning into the soft rustling of leaves and the occasional creak of branches. It was as if the trees were indeed speaking to them, sharing the wisdom of the forest.

Nanak then led the children to a gentle stream that flowed through the heart of the forest. The clear water sparkled in the sunlight, casting rippling reflections on the rocks and sand beneath.

"Water is life," he said, crouching down to cup a handful of water. "Just like the trees, the river gives freely. It provides a home for the fish, quenches our thirst, and nourishes the plants that grow along its banks. Without it, nothing could survive."

The children took turns kneeling by the river, splashing their hands and faces, feeling the refreshing coolness of the water. They observed small fish darting around, and colorful pebbles resting at the bottom.

A young boy named Kabir, who had a keen eye, noticed something shiny in the water and began to reach for it, but Nanak gently placed a hand on his shoulder.

"The river's treasures should remain in the river, Kabir," he said kindly. "Just as we wouldn't want someone to take our home, the creatures here depend on these waters. We should appreciate these gifts without disturbing their balance."

Kabir withdrew his hand, understanding the lesson. He saw that respecting nature meant leaving it as it was, so it could continue to sustain life.

As they continued their journey, Nanak pointed out various animals that inhabited the forest—birds flitting from branch to branch, squirrels gathering nuts, and a family of deer grazing peacefully nearby.

"These creatures are our brothers and sisters," he told the children. "They live in harmony with the land, taking only what they need and leaving the rest for others."

A small bird with vibrant blue feathers landed nearby, pecking at the ground. Nanak motioned for the children to sit quietly and watch.

"You see how gently the bird moves? She searches for food, but she does not take more than she needs. In her small, quiet way, she shows us respect for the gifts of the Earth."

The children were mesmerized. They hadn't thought of animals as teachers before, but they could see that each creature played its part in the forest. They watched the birds, squirrels, and deer with newfound respect, understanding that these creatures were part of a delicate balance.

Nanak then gathered the children around a small sapling growing near the edge of the forest. Its young leaves were bright green, and it swayed gently in the breeze.

"This little tree is just beginning its life," he explained, brushing his fingers over the leaves. "Someday, it will grow tall and strong, providing shade, fruit, and shelter. But for it to reach its full potential, it needs our care and protection."

Nanak handed each child a small pouch filled with seeds, encouraging them to plant their own trees in the forest. "When we plant a tree, we give something back to the Earth. It's a way of saying thank you for all the gifts it has given us."

The children eagerly dug small holes in the soil, placing the seeds gently into the ground. They covered each seed with soil, patting it down carefully. They felt a sense of pride, knowing they were contributing to the forest's future.

"By planting these seeds, you become caretakers of this land," Nanak told them. "The forest will remember your kindness and continue to thrive, offering its gifts to future generations."

Before they left the forest, Nanak gathered the children in a circle under a large, ancient tree. He explained the interconnectedness of life, how each element of nature—soil, water, plants, animals, and even people—was part of a larger circle.

"The Earth, the sky, the rivers, and all living beings are connected," he said. "When we take care of one, we care for all. But when we harm one, it affects everyone."

The children sat quietly, absorbing his words. They understood now that their actions mattered, that they had a responsibility to protect and respect the world around them.

Nanak ended their journey with a gentle reminder: "The gifts of the Earth and sky are precious. If we treat them with love and care, they will continue to bless us. Let us always remember to walk gently on this Earth, for it is our shared home."

As the children left the forest, they felt a deep sense of gratitude for the natural world. They carried with them the lessons of the ants, the trees, the river, and the animals, vowing to live with respect and kindness toward nature.

The experience left a lasting impact on them, inspiring them to share these lessons with others. They became young stewards of the Earth, encouraging their families and friends to cherish and protect the natural world.

Through Nanak's gentle teachings, the children had not only learned about the beauty and wisdom of nature but had also developed a sense of responsibility for the gifts of Earth and sky.

Chapter 14: Wings of Forgiveness

One peaceful afternoon, Nanak sat under a shady tree in the village square, strumming the familiar, gentle notes of his beloved rabab. His music drifted through the air, creating a soothing melody that made everyone around feel calm and happy. Children gathered close by, listening intently as Nanak played, each one enchanted by the soft, flowing sound.

Among them was a boy named Karan, who admired Nanak deeply and loved listening to his songs. Karan was a bit shy and clumsy, but he was kind-hearted and always tried to help where he could. That day, as he moved closer to see the rabab, he stumbled over a loose stone. Before he knew it, he had tripped forward, landing right on the precious instrument with a loud *crack!*

Everyone froze. The once soothing music stopped abruptly, and all eyes turned to the rabab, now lying in Karan's hands, its strings snapped and one wooden piece cracked. A hush fell over the children as they looked at the broken instrument, then at Karan, and finally at Nanak, wondering what he would say.

Karan's face turned red with embarrassment and fear. "I... I didn't mean to..." he stammered, clutching the broken pieces, his hands shaking. He was filled with regret and worry, his heart sinking as he imagined how much trouble he might be in.

Nanak looked at the broken instrument, then at Karan's tear-filled eyes. For a brief moment, he was silent. But instead of anger or frustration, his face softened into a gentle smile. He reached out, placing a comforting hand on Karan's shoulder.

"It's alright, Karan," he said kindly. "I know you didn't mean to break it. Things happen by accident sometimes."

Karan blinked, surprised by Nanak's calmness. He expected Nanak to be upset, maybe even disappointed. After all, the rabab

GURU NANAK'S WAY: LESSONS FOR YOUNG HEARTS 65

was something special to him, a beloved companion in his journey of music and devotion. But here Nanak was not a trace of anger in his eyes, only kindness and understanding.

"But... your rabab... it's broken," Karan whispered, still feeling terrible.

Nanak took the broken pieces from Karan's hands and looked at them thoughtfully. "This rabab has brought much joy, and it will again," he said gently. "But what matters most is not the instrument itself—it's the music it carries and the love we feel when we share it. Forgiveness is like that love. When we forgive, we create more space in our hearts for peace and joy."

The other children listened, fascinated. They hadn't thought about forgiveness in this way before. To them, forgiveness was something grown-ups talked about, but now, they could see it as something simple and real—a way to feel lighter and happier.

As Nanak spoke, the children began to understand that forgiveness wasn't just about saying "it's okay" when someone makes a mistake. Forgiveness was about freeing oneself from the weight of anger or sadness. Nanak explained it in a way that made perfect sense to them.

"Imagine you're carrying a big stone in your heart," Nanak said, using his hands to mimic holding something heavy. "If someone hurts you, the stone gets bigger and heavier. But when you forgive, it's like letting that stone go, and suddenly, your heart feels light, like it could float."

The children closed their eyes, trying to imagine this. It was as if they could see themselves holding heavy stones, weighed down by small hurts or misunderstandings. Then they imagined letting go, feeling the warmth of forgiveness lifting them up like wings.

"Forgiveness is like growing wings," Nanak continued. "With forgiveness, we're no longer held down by anger. We can soar, just like birds in the sky."

Karan listened, feeling a mixture of relief and happiness. He felt the warmth of Nanak's forgiveness surrounding him, lifting the weight of his guilt. In that moment, he felt as if he, too, had grown wings.

After the incident with the rabab, the children went about their day, reflecting on what they had learned. Nanak continued to talk to them about forgiveness, sharing small stories of times when people around him had chosen kindness over anger, or understanding over frustration.

One child, a girl named Leela, raised her hand, curious. "But Bhai Nanak," she asked, "what if someone hurts us on purpose? Isn't it hard to forgive then?"

Nanak nodded, acknowledging her question. "Yes, sometimes it's very hard to forgive, especially if someone has been unkind on purpose. But remember, forgiveness doesn't mean we forget or allow someone to keep hurting us. It means we choose not to carry the weight of that hurt in our hearts. We let it go so that we can find peace."

He looked at each child, his expression warm and encouraging. "Forgiveness is like a gift we give to ourselves. It helps us move forward and leaves more room for happiness in our hearts."

The children wanted to practice what they had learned. They decided to take on a "forgiveness challenge" for the week, where each of them would try to forgive someone for a small mistake and see how it made them feel. They shared their experiences, from forgiving a friend who accidentally knocked over their lunch, to forgiving a sibling who borrowed something without asking.

One by one, they discovered that forgiving was not only kind but also made them feel lighter, just as Nanak had said. Each child shared a small story about how forgiving helped them feel happier and brought them closer to their friends and family.

As the week passed, they noticed that little arguments and misunderstandings seemed to disappear more quickly. They began to see forgiveness as a magical way to keep their hearts open and happy.

A few days later, the children surprised Nanak with a thoughtful gift. They had gathered materials and, with the help of some adults, worked together to repair his rabab. They brought it to him, their faces beaming with pride.

"Bhai Nanak," Karan said, holding out the beautifully restored instrument, "we wanted to fix your rabab to show how much we've learned from you. Just as you forgave me for breaking it, we all want to remember to forgive others, too."

Nanak accepted the rabab, deeply moved by the children's gesture. He strummed it softly, and a beautiful melody filled the air once again. The children listened, feeling that the music sounded even sweeter than before, filled with the spirit of forgiveness and love.

With a warm smile, Nanak told them, "You see, forgiveness has brought us even closer together. And just like this rabab, when we forgive, we create harmony. We let our hearts sing."

The story of Nanak and the broken rabab soon spread throughout the village. The adults were amazed by the wisdom of the children, who had not only learned but were now teaching others about the power of forgiveness. People began to notice how the children interacted, letting go of small disagreements and choosing understanding over anger.

Over time, even the adults began practicing forgiveness more often, inspired by Nanak's message and the children's example. The entire village felt lighter, as if everyone had grown invisible wings that lifted their spirits and brought them closer.

Through Nanak's gentle guidance, the children—and the entire village—came to realize that forgiveness was not a weakness but a powerful act that created peace and joy. They learned that forgiveness was a gift that everyone could give, a gift that made hearts lighter and brighter.

With this lesson, Nanak had given the children a lifelong tool for happiness. They understood that life would sometimes bring misunderstandings or moments of hurt, but with forgiveness, they could always find their way back to peace. Forgiveness, they saw, was like an invisible pair of wings, lifting them above any troubles and filling their hearts with joy.

Whenever someone in the village felt hurt or angered, the children would remind them of Nanak's words: "Forgiveness is like wings that lift us up and help us fly free."

And from that day on, whenever the children listened to Nanak's music, they felt not just the beauty of the melody but also the gentle power of forgiveness that held them all together, like a quiet, unseen song.

Chapter 15: Walking Together

As the sun cast its warm, golden light over the village, Guru Nanak Dev Ji sat beneath a large banyan tree in the village square, surrounded by his friends, family, and many children who had come to see him. The people gathered knew that Nanak was preparing to embark on another journey, one that would take him far from their village. His teachings had become deeply woven into their lives, guiding them toward kindness, understanding, and unity.

But today was special. Nanak had called everyone together, young and old, for one last time. He wanted to share a final message with them, something they could carry with them, no matter where they were. The children, in particular, gathered closely, eager to hear what he had to say.

With his serene smile, Nanak looked around at the eager faces, his heart brimming with love for each of them. He knew that every person, young or old, had the capacity to bring light into the world.

"My dear friends," Nanak began, his voice gentle yet clear, "over the years, we have shared many beautiful moments together. We have learned about kindness, forgiveness, love, and courage. But there is one thing I want each of you to remember above all."

He looked at the children, his eyes sparkling. "Each of you is like a little light. No matter how small you may feel, you have the power to make the world brighter. Just like a candle that can light up a dark room, your actions, no matter how small, can bring warmth and happiness to others."

The children listened closely, some nodding, others holding their breath. Nanak's words made them feel special, as though they each carried a hidden spark within them that could change the world.

"If you carry love and kindness in your heart," he continued, "then everywhere you go, you will spread light. And as more people join you in spreading kindness, the world will become brighter and more joyful. This is how we walk together."

The children looked around at one another, as though seeing each other in a new light. They began to understand that they were all part of something greater—a path of love, kindness, and unity that they could walk together.

"But Bhai Nanak," a boy named Amar asked, his voice filled with curiosity, "how can we always walk together? Won't we be in different places?"

Nanak nodded, smiling at Amar's thoughtful question. "Yes, you may find yourselves in different places, facing different challenges. But walking together doesn't mean you have to be side by side. It means you carry the same values in your hearts, wherever you go. When you choose kindness, you walk with me. When you choose honesty, forgiveness, and love, you walk together with everyone who shares those values."

He took a deep breath, feeling the warmth of the crowd's attention. "Imagine each of us as a little light. Alone, we might seem small, but when we join together, we become a great, shining light that can brighten even the darkest places."

To help them understand his message, Nanak began sharing a few stories from his journeys, stories of people who had chosen kindness, honesty, and courage even when it was difficult. Each story illustrated how one act of love or compassion could create a ripple effect, spreading from person to person like light moving through the darkness.

In one story, he spoke of a traveler who shared his food with a stranger on a stormy night, even though he had little to spare. This simple act of kindness sparked a friendship that lasted a lifetime. In another story, he told of a woman who forgave her friend's harsh words and, in doing so, healed a friendship that had been broken.

"Every small act of kindness," Nanak explained, "adds up to a world filled with love and compassion. When you choose to be kind, you are not just helping one person; you are creating a wave of goodness that can reach far beyond what you can see."

The children absorbed each story, realizing that they, too, could be part of these ripples of kindness. Even the smallest actions, they now saw, could grow into something greater than themselves.

Nanak then asked the children to close their eyes for a moment and think about the world they wanted to create—a world filled with kindness, joy, and unity. "Imagine," he said softly, "a place where everyone cares for one another, where no one feels alone, and where every heart shines like a light."

The children smiled, imagining this beautiful place. Then Nanak continued, "If each of us promises to bring even a little of this dream into our lives, we can make it real. We can walk together in this dream, helping one another, sharing our gifts, and lifting each other up."

Nanak's words inspired the children, who felt eager to make this promise. One by one, they raised their hands, promising to carry love, kindness, and unity in their hearts wherever they went.

The adults, too, joined in, inspired by the children's enthusiasm. Soon, it wasn't just the children but the entire village promising to live by the values Nanak had taught them. They felt connected, united by a shared purpose and by the love and kindness that Nanak had instilled in them.

Nanak knew that this gathering would be one of his last with the villagers. His journey was calling him onward, but he felt a deep peace knowing that his teachings would continue to live on in the hearts of those he loved.

Before they parted, he left them with one final thought: "Remember, the journey we walk is a journey of the heart. It is a journey that does not end, no matter where we go or how far we travel. As long as we walk with love and kindness, we are never truly apart."

The children held onto his words, feeling a deep sense of peace and purpose. They knew that no matter where life took them, they could carry Nanak's teachings with them, lighting the way for themselves and others.

As the sun began to set, casting a warm glow over the gathering, Nanak gave each child a small, handcrafted lamp. It was a simple lamp, made of clay, with a tiny wick ready to be lit. The children held their lamps carefully, understanding that they represented the light of kindness and compassion that Nanak had taught them to carry.

"When you light this lamp," Nanak told them, "remember that you are a part of something beautiful. You are a light in this world, just as each of you is a part of this circle of love. Whenever you feel lost or unsure, let this light remind you of the kindness, unity, and courage that live within you."

The children looked at their lamps with awe, feeling as though they had been entrusted with a precious treasure. They knew that the light from these lamps would help guide them, not only in their own lives but in the lives of others as well.

As the gathering came to an end, the villagers knew that it was time for Nanak to continue his journey. There were tears and smiles, hugs and heartfelt farewells, as they expressed their gratitude for all he had shared with them. They felt a deep love for Nanak, knowing that he would always be with them in spirit.

With one last smile, Nanak looked at his beloved friends, family, and especially the children who had learned so much from him. "Remember," he said, "we are always walking together, as long as we walk with love."

The children waved, holding their lamps close, their hearts full of joy and peace. They knew that Nanak's light would guide them, no matter where they went or what they faced. They understood that they were part of a larger journey, one that connected them with others through kindness, love, and unity.

After Nanak departed, the villagers continued to honor his teachings. The children passed down the values of kindness and unity to their younger siblings, cousins, and friends, ensuring that Nanak's light would never fade.

The small clay lamps became treasured keepsakes, passed down through generations, each one a reminder of Nanak's message and the promise the children had made. They would gather every year, lighting their lamps and telling stories of Guru Nanak Dev Ji, keeping his spirit alive in their hearts and lives.

In this way, Nanak's journey continued, his teachings growing like seeds in the hearts of each new generation. And in villages and towns far and wide, where people had heard of Guru Nanak's wisdom, his light shone brightly, connecting all those who chose to walk the path of love, kindness, and unity.

As the story of Guru Nanak Dev Ji draws to a close, the teachings he shared remain in the hearts of all those he touched. Though he traveled far and wide, meeting people from every walk of life, the simple truths he lived by—kindness, love, honesty, and unity—resonate as brightly today as they did then.

Guru Nanak's journey was never just his own; it was a journey meant to inspire others to find the light within themselves. He showed us that no matter where we are or who we are, each of us has the power to make the world a better place through our actions, our words, and our love. He taught that even the smallest acts of kindness can ripple outward, like the gentle waves of a calm lake, reaching far beyond what we can see.

This book, though filled with stories from long ago, is a guide for each of us today. Every child, every adult, and every heart that reads these pages becomes part of Guru Nanak's legacy—a legacy of compassion and understanding that knows no boundaries of age, place, or time. His teachings are simple yet powerful: be kind, be truthful, forgive often, and see everyone as equal. With these as our guiding lights, we can find peace within ourselves and bring peace to the world around us.

As you finish these pages, remember that the story of kindness, love, and unity is one that never truly ends. Every time you lend a helping hand, share a smile, or listen with an open heart, you are carrying forward the message of Guru Nanak Dev Ji. You are walking in his footsteps, adding your own light to his path.

So, let us all be like the little lights Nanak spoke of, brightening the world with each step. Let us carry his teachings in our hearts, and may his journey inspire us to keep walking, together, toward a world filled with love, joy, and peace.

The End of the Book, but the Beginning of a Journey

Don't miss out!

Visit the website below and you can sign up to receive emails whenever Aariv Wadhwa publishes a new book. There's no charge and no obligation.

https://books2read.com/r/B-A-URNSC-IICHF

BOOKS2READ

Connecting independent readers to independent writers.

Did you love *Guru Nanak's Way: Lessons for Young Hearts*? Then you should read *Veil of Vision: The Third Eye*[1] by Aariv Wadhwa!

Veil of Vision: The Third Eye is a story of inner discovery, courage, and transformation. In a world where everyone is born with a dormant third eye that awakens only through great emotional upheaval, we follow the journey of Mahadev, a young man who stumbles upon a gift he never asked for. This gift, however, is feared by society. The ability to perceive beyond what is ordinary reveals the true nature of those around him—and this knowledge, as Mahadev discovers, is both powerful and dangerous.

This story is an exploration of the challenges that come with understanding others on a deeper level. It reminds us of the responsibility that accompanies any unique talent or gift. As Mahadev struggles to keep his powers hidden and ultimately decides to use them for good, he learns about

---

1. https://books2read.com/u/m09BwM

2. https://books2read.com/u/m09BwM

acceptance, compassion, and courage. I hope that his journey resonates with readers and serves as a reminder that, often, the greatest truths are found beneath the surface.

The third eye is an ancient concept, often representing an eye beyond our physical sight. Throughout history, different cultures have spoken of a deeper vision, a way of seeing that reveals truths hidden from ordinary eyes. In Veil of Vision: The Third Eye, the third eye symbolizes our ability to perceive, understand, and act with wisdom.

Mahadev, lives in a society where everyone possesses the potential for this vision. Yet, only a rare few ever experience it fully, as it can only be awakened through intense emotional experiences. In Mahadev's world, people have been conditioned to fear this sight, to reject it as something unnatural or even dangerous. Yet, Mahadev's journey teaches us that sometimes, our fears keep us from seeing the beauty and responsibility that lie within us.

Through Mahadev's awakening, we are invited to ask ourselves questions about perspective, empathy, and the importance of understanding others at a deeper level. This story is not just about Mahadev's journey to control his vision, but also about his quest to find acceptance and purpose.

Veil of Vision: The Third Eye is, at its heart, a story of courage, self-acceptance, and the realization that sometimes our greatest challenges lead us to our greatest strengths. As you turn the pages, I hope you, too, find new ways of seeing the world—and yourself.

Enjoy the journey!